A to Z
ANIMALS
Around the World

Grosset & Dunlap, Publishers

Here's a book that tells you about many animals from all over the world. From alligator to zebra, there's an animal for each letter of the alphabet. So start reading! You'll discover where 26 animals live and play. There's also a poster of the world with stickers to hang in your room. You can put the animal stickers on the place where each animal lives.

Special thanks to James G. Doherty, General Curator, Bronx Zoo, Wildlife Conservation Park.

Text copyright © 1994 by Grosset & Dunlap, Inc. Illustrations copyright © 1994 by Bettina Paterson.
All rights reserved. Published by Grosset & Dunlap, Inc., a member of The Putnam & Grosset Group, New York.
GROSSET & DUNLAP is a trademark of Grosset & Dunlap, Inc.
Published simultaneously in Canada. Printed in the U.S.A. ISBN 0-448-40474-5 LOC: 93-78935
A B C D E F G H I J

A to Z
ANIMALS
Around the World

By Alexandra E. Fischer
Illustrated by Bettina Paterson

A alligator

Alligators are reptiles. They have dry, scaly skin. They lay eggs. They breathe air through lungs. And like most reptiles, they live in warm places. The American alligator lives in the swamps, lakes, and rivers of the southern part of the United States.

B bear

These are Alaskan brown bears. They live in the northern part of America. There are many different kinds of bears. Some look cute and cuddly. Some can even be trained to do tricks. But all bears can be dangerous, especially a female who thinks someone is trying to hurt her cubs.

C camel

Arabian camels have one hump. Bactrian camels have two. Why do camels have humps at all? The humps store fat which the camel can use for energy when there isn't much food to eat. This Arabian camel lives in the hot, dry deserts of Africa, where there is hardly any water. So it's a good thing camels don't get thirsty very often. In fact, they can go for weeks without a drink.

D dolphin

Dolphins look like fish, but they aren't. They have lungs, breathe air, and give birth to live babies. They are mammals—like dogs and elephants, and you! There are dolphins in all of the oceans of the world. But this pretty white-sided dolphin lives only in the North Atlantic Ocean.

E elephant

The elephant is the largest animal that lives on land. There are two kinds of elephants. African elephants have large ears and long legs. This baby is an Asian, or Indian elephant. You can tell because it has small ears and short legs.

F flamingo

Flamingos eat lots of shrimp and other small water
animals. They scoop water up and then pump it through
strainers in their bills, so that just the food is left for
them to swallow. Flamingos like to stay near the water
in large groups. These bright coral flamingos live in the
Caribbean Sea.

G giraffe

Giraffes are often found among the trees on the African savannas. They like to nibble at leaves and twigs and fruit high off the ground. The trees also help to hide giraffes from enemies like lions.

H hippopotamus

Hippos love water! In fact, they may spend up to half of their lives just floating around in the rivers and lakes of Africa. For this reason, many people think that hippos are lazy and slow. But that's not true. Hippos can actually run as fast as people can.

I iguana

Did you know that iguanas can swim? They can! These reptiles are usually found in tree branches near river-banks in Central and South America. But if an enemy comes too near, the iguana can jump into the water and swim away!

J jaguar

Jaguars live in Central and South America. Like most cats, they like to hunt at night. During the day, they rest. The spots on a jaguar make it blend into the bushes or leaves around it, so jaguars stay hidden while they are asleep. There are also black jaguars, but they are very rare.

K koala

Koalas, which live in Australia, are often called koala bears. But they are not really bears. They are marsupials. Marsupials are animals like kangaroos, that carry their babies in pouches. The word "koala" means "no drink." And these cuddly-looking animals don't drink any water. They get their water from the leaves of the eucalyptus tree.

L lion

Lions are among the biggest cats on earth. They live in groups called prides in the woods and plains of parts of Africa. Lions can often be seen dozing in the tall grass. They have been known to spend up to twenty hours a day sleeping!

M mandrill

There are more than two hundred kinds of monkeys! This one is a mandrill. You can tell it is a full-grown male because of its brightly colored face. It is easy for other mandrills in the group to keep sight of him as he leads them through the thick forests of western Africa.

N numbat

There is more about numbats that we *don't* know than we *do* know. There aren't many numbats left in the world, but nobody is sure what made them disappear. We are not even sure how many are left! We do know that numbats are ant-eating marsupials. They grow only to be a foot long. They can still be found in some forests of Australia.

O owl

This is a snowy owl. It lives in the very northern part of America and way up in the Arctic near the North Pole. Its white color makes it hard to see in the snow. That's important if there is a hungry fox or wolf nearby.

P penguin

Penguins are odd birds. They are great swimmers, but they can't fly. And so they build their nests on the hard ground instead of in trees. They have flippers instead of wings, and they like to swim in cold water. The Antarctic, where it never gets warm, is the perfect home for the emperor penguin.

Q quail

Quails, like penguins, build their nests in hollows in the ground. But quails like to live in meadows and cornfields instead of near the water. And quails are birds that like to hide. Often the only way to know that a quail is nearby is by hearing its call. There are many different kinds of quails all over the world. This one lives in Europe.

R reindeer

When you think of reindeer, you probably think of Santa Claus. Reindeer actually do pull sleighs—they live in places like Lapland, far, far north, and are very helpful to the people there. They can pull loaded sleighs quickly for long distances. Farmers get milk, cheese, and many other products from reindeer.

S snake

This is one of the largest snakes in the world. It is an anaconda, and it lives in South America. An anaconda may grow to be nearly thirty feet long—as long as three cars! Snakes like the anaconda wrap themselves around an animal to stop it from breathing. Then they open their jaws very wide and swallow the animal whole— no chewing!

T tortoise

Tortoises are turtles that live on land. So, instead of having flippers, they have legs. They have a high, round shell that protects them. It must work well, because some tortoises live to be more than one hundred years old! The Galapagos tortoise is one of the largest tortoises in the world. It lives in the Galapagos Islands off the coast of South America.

U umbrella bird

The umbrella bird of South America gets its name from that unusual tuft of feathers on its head. This male umbrella bird has black feathers with blue edges, while the female is a plain brown color. Most male birds are more colorful than females. They use their beautiful feathers to attract a mate.

vampire bat

This is a vampire bat. From far away it looks like a bird. But it isn't. Like all bats, it's a mammal. The vampire bat lives in Central and South America. While most bats eat a lot of insects, vampire bats feed on the blood of cattle, horses, and other animals. Don't worry, though, they hardly ever come near people.

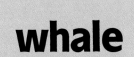

whale

Whales, like dolphins, are mammals. They have lungs just like people do. And even though baby whales are born underwater, their mothers have to push them to the top of the ocean so they can take their first breath of air.

The blue whale is the largest animal the world has ever seen. It can grow to be one hundred feet long. And in one day a blue whale may eat up to forty million krill, which are tiny sea creatures. Blue whales can live in any part of the world, but they have been hunted so much that they are now very rare.

X

x-ray fish

Scientists call this tiny fish (the biggest are under two inches long) by a very big name—*Pristella maxillaris*. But it's also known as an X-ray fish. It got its nickname because you can sometimes see right through it! This fish comes from South America, where it lives in the Amazon River.

Y yak

This is a yak. It lives on the high cold plateaus of Tibet, in Asia. This shaggy animal is very similar to the ox. Yaks, like oxen, can be tamed. And in Tibet, they help people carry things—even the mail. People there also get their milk from yaks.

Z zebra

Zebras look sort of like horses, except they have stripes. When zebras are feeding in the tall grasses of Africa, their stripes help hide them from lions. When zebras are standing in a group, it's hard to see where one ends and another starts. Unlike horses, zebras are hard to tame. That's why nobody goes zebra-back riding!